# School
# Campout

**Other books in the
Shooting Star series:**

The Big Race!
by Sylvia McNicoll

My Homework is in the Mail!
by Becky Citra

The Lost Locket
by Carol Matas

Abra Kadabra
by Maureen Bayless

Howard's House is Haunted
by Maureen Bayless

Mystery of the Lunchbox Criminal
by Alison Lohans

The Secret Plan
by Alison Lohans

Project Disaster
by Sylvia McNicoll

Monsters in the School
by Martyn Godfrey

Adventure in Legoland
by Carol Matas

# School Campout

**Becky Citra**

Illustrations by
**Susan Gardos**

**Scholastic Canada Ltd.**

*To Mark, Andrew, Michael and Brian.*

**Canadian Cataloguing in Publication Data**

Citra, Becky
    School campout

(Shooting star)
ISBN 0-590-24920-7

I. Title.    II. Series.

PS8555.I87S3  1996            jC813'.54            C96-930929-5
PZ7.C57Sc  1996

 6 5 4 3 2 1            Printed in Canada            6 7 8 9/9

# Contents

# Chapter 1

# The Surprise

"D<sub>avey</sub>..."

David hunched his shoulders. He ducked through the doorway of the grade three classroom.

"Daaavey!"

David slung his jacket on his coat hook. He took a deep breath and let it out slowly. If only that new kid, Bradley, would leave him alone.

It had all started two weeks earlier. Mr. Foster had put Bradley's desk next to David's.

"David was new this year, too," he'd said. "He knows what it feels like." David had tried to smile.

Inside, his stomach made a knot. It had taken him a long time to feel like part of the class. But he had friends now. Guys like Jason and Matt and Jonathan. Getting stuck with Bradley would wreck everything.

A jacket and a lunch kit thudded on the floor beside David. Bradley's face was red from running. "Hi, Davey. I guess you didn't hear me calling you."

David frowned. He'd told Bradley a hundred times to call him *David*, not Davey. He probably thought it was some kind of stupid joke. Or else he was too dumb to remember.

David picked up his backpack. Oh no! Something was dripping from the corner. His Thermos was leaking. Great! So far, this was turning out to be a terrible day.

Bradley opened his lunch kit and took out an

apple. He took a big bite. "Mr. Foster's going to tell us about the surprise, today."

David's stomach did a flip-flop. Mr. Foster was not a normal teacher. He had a bushy red beard like a lumberjack. He snowshoed around the playground in the winter. He taught the class how to tie fishing flies in Art. He thought up dangerous surprises.

David looked at Bradley. He was munching on a tuna-fish sandwich now. Hadn't he had breakfast?

"I bet the surprise will be good," said Bradley, through a mouthful of sandwich.

"I bet it will be terrible!" said David. "You'll see!"

Bradley stopped chewing and stared at David.

"All Mr. Foster's surprises are terrible," said David. He forgot that most of the kids in the class liked the surprises. "You know what he did in the winter? He brought a rotten old stump inside. And because it was warm, all these gross bugs came crawling out. They were everywhere! When you walked to the pencil sharpener, all you could hear was CRUNCH CRUNCH CRUNCH!"

Bradley grinned.

David jabbed his finger at Bradley's sandwich. "There were even bugs in our food!"

"Oh," said Bradley. He stopped smiling. David turned away in disgust. He carried his dripping backpack to the sink and dumped out the Thermos. He glanced around the classroom. Some of the grade threes were by the bulletin board, huddled around Jason. Jason always attracted a crowd.

David hurried to the bulletin board.

Jason looked up. "Hi, Davey!" he teased.

The kids laughed. David's cheeks turned red. Bradley was making him look like a dope. He peered over Jason's shoulder so that he wouldn't have to look at anyone.

Mr. Foster had tacked some photographs on the bulletin board. David looked at one of a log house with antlers hanging over the door, and another one of a moose grazing in a field.

"These are some pictures of Wildwood Ranch," said Mr. Foster. "That's where I live."

David frowned. Lots of kids in the class lived on ranches. He didn't see what was so great about a ranch. David lived in a small, white house close to town. He liked it that way.

He heard the crunch of an apple. Bradley again. David pushed through the kids. He looked more closely at the photographs. He looked hardest at a picture of a black bear standing in front of the log house. He shuddered. He wondered if the bear was real. It looked real.

Mr. Foster tugged on his red beard. "This is the surprise. We're all going to camp overnight at Wildwood Ranch."

Most of the kids cheered. David didn't. The kids asked lots of questions.

"Will we sleep in tents?"

"Can we have a campfire?"

"Am I allowed to bring my Walkman?"

David walked to his desk. He slumped in his chair and took out his book. He pretended to read. His head was buzzing.

How could everyone be so excited? Didn't they know how dangerous it was?

David knew. He'd read books about camping in the wilderness. In *Survival*, a boy fell over a cliff and broke his leg and had to eat berries for a week. And in *Lonely Lake*, a grizzly bear chased a whole family up a tree.

David's mouth felt dry. He licked his lips nervously. He stared out the window. Just two more weeks until summer holidays. Then he'd be out of grade three for good. If he lasted that long.

Just before home time, Mr. Foster handed everyone a pink notice. "This is your permission slip for the trip. Ask your parents to sign it, then bring it back as soon as possible. If you don't bring it back, you can't go."

David felt a glimmer of hope. His mom was pretty protective. She was always nagging him about zipping up his jacket and not getting his feet wet. She'd think camping was dangerous, too.

Jason waited while David put on his outside

shoes. "Let's make sure we get to stay in the same tent."

"Okay," said David. He didn't want to tell Jason he probably wasn't going. Jason would think he was crazy.

"Don't forget your notices," said Mr. Foster. "Remember. No permission slip, no trip."

David crumpled the notice in his backpack. The more he thought about it, the more positive he felt. Mom would say no.

# Chapter 2

# Tent Buddies

A few days later, Mr. Foster asked everyone to sit at their desks. He wrote CAMP RULES on the blackboard. "Does anyone have any suggestions?" he asked.

"Stay with the group," said Sarah.

"Excellent!" said Mr. Foster. "You don't want to get lost."

"Don't eat mushrooms," said Matt. "They could make you sick."

David wondered if Bradley was listening. His

cheeks were pink and he was waving his hand in the air.

David's eyes wandered to the pile of pink permission slips on the edge of Mr. Foster's desk. He still couldn't believe his mom had said yes. She'd even laughed when he'd told her about the photograph of the bear. Mom had a strange sense of humour.

The list of rules on the blackboard grew. When it was Bradley's turn, he beamed at the class. "Carry a survival kit. I brought one for Show and Tell."

Everyone laughed. Jason rolled his eyes at David. Bradley didn't know that grade threes don't call it Show and Tell anymore. David glanced sideways at Bradley. He'd hate it if everyone laughed at him. But Bradley was laughing, too.

Mr. Foster smiled. "Let's save your survival kit for Sharing Time on Thursday, Brad. It sounds great. How about if everyone tries to bring in something we can use for camping?"

David sighed. He'd planned to bring his new

remote-control racing car. Looking at a bunch of camping stuff would be boring.

Next, Mr. Foster wrote TENT BUDDIES on the blackboard. Hands shot up. Mr. Foster drew lots of triangles. In each triangle, he wrote the names of kids who wanted to sleep in the same tent.

Jonathan raised his hand. "My dad's letting me bring his bird blind," he said. "It's like a tent. He uses it for photography. It's made out of camouflage material. It's got spy holes and everything."

"Fantastic!" said Mr. Foster. He drew a big triangle and printed Jonathan's name in it.

"Jason and Matt are staying in my bird blind, too," said Jonathan. Mr. Foster added their names.

David was surprised. He raised his hand. "I'd like to be in that tent," he said.

"You can't," said Jonathan. "We've got enough already."

David turned around and stared at Jason. Jason was doodling on the top of his pencil box. He didn't look up.

"It's okay," said Bradley. "Davey can stay with me. I've got a huge tent. I got it for camping with the Cubs."

"Well, David?" said Mr. Foster.

David stared at the blackboard. His heart thumped. He hadn't been paying that much attention. Were all the boys' names up already? What if he got stuck with some of the girls?

"I guess so," he said. His voice sounded like it was coming out of a long tunnel.

"Can tent buddies sit together at lunch time today?" asked Lesley.

"Great idea!" said Mr. Foster.

When the bell rang, Bradley pushed his desk right against David's. He spread out his lunch. He had a juice box, plastic containers filled with celery and carrots and dip, several lumpy packages wrapped in waxed paper and a little round tin of chocolate pudding.

"Only three more days till the trip," said Bradley. He crunched on a stick of celery. "We'd better make some plans."

David chewed his peanut butter sandwich

slowly. It tasted like cardboard. Three more days — he didn't need Bradley reminding him. Maybe he could get sick or something. In fact, he felt a little sick now, just thinking about it.

"I'm not really hungry," he mumbled. "I'm going outside."

Bradley's face fell. David sighed. "Here, you can have my jelly doughnut."

"Hey, thanks a lot," said Bradley.

Bradley looked so happy over a dumb doughnut. David wished he could take it back. Now Bradley would think he was his friend for sure.

David folded his sandwich papers and stuck them in his backpack. Jason stopped beside his desk on his way to the garbage can. "Sorry about the tent," he said casually. "It's just that there isn't enough room. I didn't know Mr. Foster would put you with Bradley."

David's cheeks turned red. Bradley was busy unwrapping a package of cookies. David hoped he hadn't heard Jason.

"It's okay," said David. "I don't care."

But he did care. He'd felt like part of the group, until Bradley came. Now it was like being new all over again.

# Chapter 3

# Survival

On Thursday, almost everyone had something to show at Sharing Time. When it was Jason's turn, he held out his fist for a while. Then he opened it.

"TA-DAAAA!" It was a Swiss Army knife. He unfolded three small blades, a pair of miniature scissors and a tiny corkscrew.

"Wow!" said Matt. "I bet that would cut anything!"

"SWOOOSH!" said Jason. He swung his arm through the air.

"Where's the can opener?" asked Jonathan. "Swiss Army knives are supposed to have can openers."

Jason shrugged. "It broke off. So what?"

The class passed Jason's knife around the circle. David thought it was neat, even if it didn't have a can opener.

Matt showed the class his grandfather's canteen. His grandfather had used it in the army. Lesley had a metal plate, knife, fork and spoon that folded up into a kit.

It was Bradley's turn next.

One by one, he took things out of a small nylon pouch. Matches dipped in thick wax. A Power bar so you wouldn't starve. A tiny sewing kit with five different colours of thread and two white buttons. Tin foil. A compass.

David held his breath. How many other things were crammed in there? It was better than a magic trick. Bradley was digging in the pouch and humming. He pulled out a small package: "Space blanket."

The class passed all the things from Bradley's survival kit around the circle. Their voices buzzed with excitement.

Jason snapped his Swiss Army knife shut. He flipped it in the air. "Who needs a dumb survival kit?" he said in a loud voice. "I can take care of myself."

David put his hand up. He was going to tell the class about the boy in *Survival*. Bradley's kit would have helped him a lot.

"Yes?" said Mr. Foster.

Jason gave David a funny look. David changed his mind. "Nothing," he said.

Mr. Foster waited a minute. Then he said, "When Bradley mentioned his survival kit on Monday, it gave me a great idea. We're going to make survival kits for everybody." He grinned. "Even you, Jason."

Mr. Foster passed out orange garbage bags, plastic whistles, granola bars and Band-Aids. He showed the kids how to cut a hole on the

front of their bags.

"This is your survival suit. If you get lost, wear it. The hole is for your face. The bag will keep you warm and dry and the orange colour will show up from a long way away."

When they had cut their holes, the kids tried on their bags. David felt hot and sweaty in his. He tore the hole a little when he tugged it off.

Mr. Foster gave everyone a Ziploc bag. "Put your things in here. And remember, carry your survival kit on all our hikes."

* * *

That night, Mom and Dad helped David pack his gear in a duffel bag. David showed them the survival kit. Mom tucked a tiny box of raisins beside the granola bar. "Extra energy," she said. Dad handed him a brown leather case. Inside was a small pair of binoculars.

"Thanks!" said David. "These are great!" He focused on the *Star Trek* poster above his dresser. "I won't even have to go very far. I can look at stuff right from the tent."

Dad looked at Mom. He said slowly, "I didn't

realize you were so scared about camping, David. Maybe I should have taken you out in the forest more."

"I'm not scared," said David. "I just don't want to go. How would you like to share a tent with Bradley?"

"I wouldn't mind at all." Dad gave David one of his serious looks. "Remember, son, you were new in September. That's a lot easier than coming into the class at the end of the school year."

Mom and Dad looked like they were waiting for David to say something. His eyes stung. They didn't understand. It hadn't been easy being new in September, either.

Finally, Dad said, "What exactly is wrong with Bradley?"

David took a big breath. "He won't leave me alone. He eats all the time. And he thinks he knows everything!"

"Hmmm," said Dad.

"I'm not the only one who says so," said David.

"Really," said Mom.

David decided to change the subject. "Maybe it will rain. Then the trip will be cancelled."

"David!" said Dad. "You're going. Dead or alive."

"Ha, ha," said David. Dad was trying to be funny. He wasn't funny. He was sick.

David climbed into bed. He rolled onto his stomach and buried his face in his pillow. The camping trip probably *would* kill him. Then they'd be sorry.

Besides, it was easy for Mom and Dad to talk. They didn't have to go.

# Chapter 4

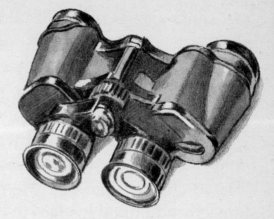

# Wildwood Ranch

$\mathbf{A}$t school the next day, a blue station wagon pulled up at the drop-off spot. Bradley got out. "Oh, no," said David.

All the kids stared. Bradley was wearing hiking boots and wool pants held up with red suspenders. A canteen dangled at his waist. Binoculars swung around his neck. A camouflage cap perched on top of his head.

Some of the kids laughed. David laughed, too, as loud as he could. Dad frowned.

"It's okay," said David. "Bradley doesn't mind."

When it was time to say goodbye to Dad, David felt a lump in his throat. He climbed aboard the school bus and sat in the front seat. There were two cardboard boxes beside him. Good. Bradley would have to sit with someone else.

The road to Wildwood Ranch wound past fields and swamps and forests. David stared out the window at the dark trees. It looked just like the kind of place bears would love.

When they arrived, Mrs. Foster was waiting on the front porch of the log house. "Welcome to Wildwood Ranch," she said. Behind the house, a river sparkled in the sun. An eagle soared over the water, its white head glistening.

"Wow!" said Bradley. "A bald eagle!" He grabbed his binoculars.

"Haven't you ever seen an eagle before?" sneered Jason.

Bradley ignored him. "It caught a fish!" he cried.

Now all the kids stared at the eagle. It was beautiful and scary at the same time. The eagle flapped its wings and soared over the tall pine trees. David let his breath out with a sigh. It was the closest he'd ever been to an eagle.

"Hey!" shouted Bradley. "Over here!" He was bending over the ground, his binoculars swinging. "Deer tracks! A deer must have walked right past here."

David's mouth dropped open. What was going on? Bradley was from the city. How come he knew so much about animals?

Jason hooted. "Ha! What makes you so sure — "

"Bradley's right," said Mr. Foster. "That deer comes by every night. Ask Mrs. Foster about it. It eats all her roses!"

Jason scowled. "Can we put up our tents?" he asked.

"Sure," said Mr. Foster. "You can put your tents anywhere in the woods by the house. When you hear three blasts of my whistle, meet me back here at the picnic table with your day packs and your lunches."

The kids spread out through the trees and grass.

"Here's a perfect spot," said Bradley. The sun shone through the trees on a flat mossy patch of ground.

"Okay," said David.

David could see Jason and Jonathan and Matt through the trees. They were arguing in loud voices. He looked away and tried to concentrate on Bradley's instructions for putting up the tent.

It seemed like there were more poles than they could ever use. The tent puffed up around them in a billowy cloud. But Bradley knew what to do. In no time at all, it popped into shape like a neat, brown mushroom.

Bradley unrolled his sleeping bag and laid it inside. He put his pack on the bottom of his bed. He hung his binoculars and canteen on a branch outside the tent.

David watched for a minute. Then he rolled

out his sleeping bag beside Bradley's. He rummaged through his duffel bag. He could feel something hard inside one of his T-shirts. A jumbo fruit and nut chocolate bar! His favourite! Mom must have snuck it in when he wasn't looking.

Bradley would probably sniff out the chocolate bar. David slipped it into his jacket pocket. He took out his flashlight and shone it on the roof of the tent. He could hear Jason and Jonathan shouting at each other.

"Hey," said Bradley sharply. "You're wasting batteries. You should turn that off."

David blinked in surprise. What was the big deal? He shrugged and flicked off the switch. Bradley was weird.

David grabbed his day pack and binoculars and crawled out of the tent. He could see the corner of Jonathan's bird blind through the trees. Giggles and excited shouts came from the other tents. David looked the other way and walked back to the river.

David threw stones in the water and waited

for the class. He looked through his binoculars and practised focusing on trees and rocks on the other side of the river. Awesome! These binoculars were the best present he'd had for a long time. Finally, Mr. Foster blew his whistle.

Jason and Jonathan and Matt were arguing loudly as they walked over to the picnic table.

"It's not my fault the tent pole broke," Jason said.

"Well, my dad's going to kill me," groaned Jonathan.

Jason grinned at David. "Guess you're pretty proud of your campsite, Davey?"

David flushed. "Bradley set it up. I didn't know how."

"Good old Bradley," said Jason.

David bit his lip. The guys would think he was sticking up for Bradley. He turned the binoculars around and peered backward at Bradley. Bradley looked small and far away.

David handed the binoculars to Jason. "Look at this."

Jason looked through the binoculars backward, too. He grinned. "Too bad they don't make Bradley disappear," he said.

The class spread out on the grass around the picnic table and ate their lunches. When they had finished, Mr. Foster handed everyone a booklet of blank pages stapled together. "This is your field book. You can get started now. You can draw and write about all the things you see on our trip."

David took his pencil crayons out of his day pack. He drew the river. He made it long and winding with big boulders and trees along the shore. Next he drew the eagle. He gave it long curved talons and a hooked beak. It was the best eagle he'd ever drawn.

David liked working in his field book. For a long time, he forgot about Jason. He forgot about Bradley. He almost didn't hear Mr. Foster.

". . . meet me here in fifteen minutes," Mr. Foster finished. "You need your survival kits and your flashlights."

David closed his field book slowly. He

followed the other kids back to the tents. His heart thumped. Flashlights? What was Mr. Foster up to now? He hurried to catch up with Jason and the others. "What's going on?" he asked.

Jason's eyes glowed. "We're going hiking and we're staying out until dark. I heard Mr. Foster telling Mrs. Foster. We're having a cookout and then coming back in the night."

David stared at Jason. It had to be a joke. Mr. Foster had taught them about nocturnal animals in Science. The animals who came out at night. The hunters. "Are you sure?" he said.

"I heard him, too," said Matt. "It's going to be cool."

David shuddered. Hiking in the forest in the middle of the night didn't sound cool to him. It sounded deadly.

# Chapter 5

# What's Wrong with Jason?

Mr. Foster heaved a backpack onto his shoulders. "Everyone follow me. And please, stay together."

"I thought we were going on a cookout," said Bradley. "Where's the food?"

The class snickered. Mr. Foster grinned. "I have enough hot dogs in here to feed an army. So there's probably enough for a grade three class, too."

The kids followed Mr. Foster along the trail.

David's binoculars bumped against the front of his shirt. He stared at the trees across the river. He hoped the eagle would come back.

After a while, the trail wound away from the river, deeper into the forest. The air smelled like pine needles. Mr. Foster said, "We're coming into a meadow. I want everyone to be very quiet. If we're lucky, we might see some sand-hill cranes."

David stepped out of the trees into the sunny meadow. He gasped. Standing in the long grass were two of the biggest birds he had ever seen.

"They have red patches on their heads," whispered Bradley, peering through his binoculars. "They're awesome."

David looked through his binoculars, too. The birds had long legs and long brown necks. He felt like he could reach out and touch them. One of the cranes turned its head. David could see its bright beady eye. It was looking right at him.

All the kids were grinning at the cranes. Their eyes shone.

"Okay," said Mr. Foster in a soft voice. "Let's

get out our field books and do a bit of work. Crouch down in the grass. Remember, no loud noises or sudden movements."

After a long time, David put down his binoculars. Bradley was sitting on the grass beside him, drawing in his field book. David opened his book. He sketched a line of tall grass at the bottom of the page. He drew the two cranes in the middle of the grass. He made them come almost to the top of the paper. With his pencil crayons, David carefully coloured light brown feathers and bright red caps on the cranes' heads.

Bradley was still working. The tip of his tongue stuck out at the corner of his mouth. David peered over his shoulder. Bradley's picture of the sandhill cranes looked real.

Bradley looked up and smiled. David shrugged. "Not bad," he said.

"Thanks," Bradley whispered. "Can I borrow some of your pencil crayons to colour it?"

David nodded. He handed Bradley his pencil case. He could feel Jason's eyes on him. Jason threw a stalk of grass and hit him on the arm.

David bent over his notebook. His cheeks felt hot. Jason gave a noisy sigh and stood up. He shut his notebook with a snap. One of the sandhill cranes swivelled its long neck toward the class.

"Sit down," said Mr. Foster quietly.

Jason stared at Mr. Foster. "Huh?"

"Shhh . . . " said the class.

Bradley leaned over and tugged the bottom of Jason's T-shirt.

"Yeow!" cried Jason. He grabbed his stomach and pretended he was shot.

*Whuump!* Jason fell to the ground with his arms and legs spread out.

The sandhill cranes flapped their long wings and lifted themselves into the air. They made a croaky sound like a rusty gate as they flew away. David bit his lip in disappointment. He could have watched the sandhill cranes forever. And now they were gone.

The class glared at Jason. Their eyes weren't shining now. They were cold.

Jason's face turned red. "It's not my fault," he said in a loud voice. "Bradley pushed me."

David opened his mouth and then shut it. It wasn't fair to blame Bradley. But he felt sorry for Jason, too. He'd feel awful if he'd been the one to scare the cranes away.

Mr. Foster led the class across the meadow and back into the forest. Jason slouched at the end of the line, his face still red. David waited for him.

"It doesn't matter," said David.

"What?" said Jason. "You don't think I care about those moron birds, do you?" He laughed rudely. "And I don't need *you* feeling sorry for me."

Jason ran ahead. David kicked a rock with his running shoe. What was wrong with Jason, anyway? He used to be a lot of fun. But since Bradley came, he'd been a real jerk.

David shook his head. Everything was getting so mixed up.

Ahead of David, the line of kids broke apart. They milled around in a circle. David could

hear Mr. Foster's excited voice. His heart
thumped hard.

Now what?

# Chapter 6

## Bradley's Secret

"Something moved this boulder," said Mr. Foster. "Any guesses?"

The boulder lay at the edge of the trail. There was a hole in the dirt beside it. Puzzled looks spread across the kids' faces. A few of them shook their heads.

Bradley put his hand up. He bounced up and down. He looked like he was going to burst.

Mr. Foster smiled. "Hang on for a sec, Brad. I want everyone to do some thinking here."

"It's a meteorite that hit the Earth," said Jason. "Pow!"

Everyone laughed. That was a pretty smart answer, thought David, even though Jason was just kidding. He wished he'd thought of it.

"Well," said Mr. Foster, "anybody want to try to roll it back?"

Everyone had a turn. They leaned against the huge rock. They shoved. They grunted and groaned. The boulder didn't budge.

Mr. Foster rubbed his beard. "So what do you think's going on here?"

David licked his lips. He said, "It must have been something pretty big."

Mr. Foster nodded.

"A bear!" said David. His voice came out in a high squeak. Some of the kids laughed. David's cheeks turned red.

Mr. Foster said, "David's right. It *was* a bear. It was looking for bugs to eat."

David glanced around nervously. That bear

must have been hungry to move a huge boulder like that. *Very* hungry. It would be dumb to think a few old bugs would fill it up.

"The bear's been working on this rotten log, too," said Mr. Foster.

"Bears eat insects and little animals that live in old logs," said Bradley. "I did a project on bears at my old school."

David stared at the chunks of orange wood torn from the middle of the log and scattered on the ground. Goose bumps prickled the back of his neck.

One of the kids asked, "What else do bears eat?"

Everyone looked at Bradley. David turned away. He didn't want to know what bears ate.

"Berries and nuts," said Bradley. He scanned the ground. "I'm going to look for bear tracks. They have five toes. Sometimes you can see the claw marks."

"Cool," said Sarah.

"Can I look, too?" said Matt.

David shivered. Bradley was probably right. He was turning out to be right about a lot of things. He tried not to let the panic show on his face. He stayed in the middle of the line as the class headed down the trail.

David remembered that in *Lonely Lake*, the father carried a tin can filled with rocks. He shook it to scare the bears away. David wished he had a tin can. He wished the kids would make more noise.

Finally, Mr. Foster stopped in a clearing beside a creek. "This is the end of the road," he said cheerfully. "Good hiking, everyone. Well done."

David slid his pack off thankfully. He was surprised when his stomach rumbled. The afternoon had flown by. But if they cooked the hot dogs right away, they might get back before it got really dark.

"When do we eat?" said Bradley.

Mr. Foster laughed. "Not yet. We have a bit of exploring to do."

David's heart sank. Mr. Foster sounded

mysterious, like he was building up to one of his surprises.

"Mrs. Foster and I made an interesting discovery last time we were out hiking. We found a bear den up in those rocks on the side of the hill."

Everyone started to talk at once.

David's mouth fell open. Mr. Foster wanted them to explore a *bear den*? Was he crazy?

"Wait a minute!" said David. He didn't mean to say it so loudly. The kids stared at him. David's cheeks turned hot. "I mean, what if there's a bear inside?"

"Bears only hibernate in dens," said Mr. Foster. "They abandon them in the spring."

"Oh," said David. He felt stupid.

Mr. Foster dug in his backpack. "It's still interesting to take a look. We'll take my big flashlight. You can take turns exploring inside."

The class scrambled up through the trees on the side of the hill. The den opening was between two huge boulders.

David hung back while the kids divided into

partners. Mr. Foster said the bears had finished hibernating. But what if some old bear got mixed up? He might be in there right now, dreaming about food. Had Mr. Foster thought about that?

"Jonathan and me are going first!" said Jason. Mr. Foster handed Jason his flashlight. The two boys stuck their heads between the boulders. They disappeared inside.

David held his breath. He tried not to look worried. But he was ready to run. After a long time, the boys crawled back out. Jason grinned at David. "There's old bones in there. And a human skull."

"Cut it out," said David.

He could see that Bradley was the only one left without a partner. He was stuck with him again. David sucked in his breath. He'd poke his head in the den and take a quick peek, that was all.

David waited until the end. Lesley and Sarah backed out. There were bits of dry leaves in their hair.

"It's awesome," said Lesley. She handed David the flashlight. "Your turn."

David got down on his hands and knees. He crawled through the small opening. Bradley crawled beside him. David turned on the flashlight.

The den widened out and was bigger than he'd thought. There were old leaves and pebbles on the ground. David poked the flashlight into the shadows. No bones.

Beside him, Bradley grunted. He wiggled further into the den. After a minute, David squeezed in with him. It was quiet and smelled musty. The kids' voices outside were muffled.

"This is cool," said Bradley. He waved his hand excitedly and bumped David's arm. David dropped the flashlight. It banged against a rock and went out.

Bradley gave a small yelp. David's heart thudded. He groped for the flashlight in the darkness. His fingers brushed through the crackly leaves and touched something fuzzy. He gulped. Bear fur?

David's hand bumped against the flashlight. He grabbed it thankfully and flicked the switch. He blinked in the sudden light and grinned at Bradley.

Bradley's eyes were huge. He hissed, "What did you do that for?"

David stopped smiling. "What do you mean? It wasn't on purpose."

Bradley ran his tongue slowly around his lips. He pressed his hands against his knees. They were shaking.

"Hey," said David. "Are you all right?"

Bradley didn't look at David. "Forget it," he mumbled.

David's eyes widened. Bradley was afraid. He was more afraid than David. Afraid of what? Not bears. Bradley liked bears.

David wiggled out backward. Bradley followed, then stood up and brushed the dirt off his knees. He walked away and stood by himself.

David frowned. Bradley had been camping lots of times. He could set up a tent faster than anyone. He could identify animal tracks. And he knew lots of stuff about bears.

David's head spun.

Bradley was afraid of the *dark*.

David hurried down the hill to catch up to Jason and the other guys. His runners skidded on the rocks.

"Hi, Davey," said Jason. "Where's your buddy?"

David flushed. "I can tell you something pretty weird about Bradley."

The boys stopped walking.

"Tell us," demanded Jason.

David glanced over his shoulder. Bradley's cap was bobbing through the trees above them.

"I will," he promised. "Later."

# Chapter 7

# Lost!

David watched his marshmallow carefully. He'd already eaten seven burnt ones. This one was turning golden brown and puffy.

Jason crammed a charcoal-black marshmallow into his mouth. He mumbled, "Did you hear about the midnight feast?"

David groaned. He was stuffed with hot dogs, cookies and marshmallows. He probably wasn't going to be hungry for ten years.

"Jonathan brought a bag of cookies," said

Jason. "Matt's got Cheesies and I've got some doughnuts."

David thought about the jumbo fruit and nut chocolate bar in his pocket. He wasn't sure he wanted to share it.

Lesley was listening. "Can Sarah and I come, too?"

"What have you got?" said Jason.

Lesley thought a moment. "Two cans of pop left from lunch. And Sarah has Ding Dongs and pretzels."

"Okay," said Jason.

Jonathan looked worried. "My dad will kill me if we spill food in his bird blind."

Jason shrugged. "We'll use Bradley's tent. It's the only one big enough anyway."

David frowned. A midnight feast in Bradley's tent was a bad idea. He'd seen how much Bradley could eat.

David looked at his perfect marshmallow. It had turned into a black lump. With a sigh, he slid it off the stick and tossed it into the campfire. He was sick of marshmallows, anyway.

Mr. Foster started telling the class a native legend about an eagle. The fire died to glowing embers. David only half listened to the story. Didn't anyone care how late it was getting? Finally, Mr. Foster filled a plastic jug with water from the creek and doused the campfire. He packed the leftover hot dogs and marshmallows in his backpack. "Everybody get ready to go," he said. "If we don't get back soon, that old bear will find us."

David gulped. Was Mr. Foster joking? David wasn't taking any chances. He zipped up his jacket and slung his binoculars around his neck. He was going to make sure he didn't get left behind.

Some of the girls started to sing softly. A few kids turned on their flashlights. David watched Bradley test his and then turn it off. He's saving his batteries, David thought. He checked to see that his flashlight was at the top of his pack so he could get it easily.

"Hey, David, come and walk with Jonathan and me," said Jason.

"Sure," said David.

The day was turning out better than he'd thought. Jason sounded like his old self again. The bald eagle and the sandhill cranes had been great. And they hadn't seen one bear. But just the same, David was glad they were going back to the tents.

David glanced back at Jason. He was bending over, tying his shoelace. His backpack leaned against a rock. David took his binoculars out of their case and practised using them while he waited for Jason.

He trained the binoculars slowly across the bushes at the edge of the clearing. He saw something move in a clump of tall grass. David held the binoculars still. He looked more closely.

Nothing.

He was about to turn away when the grass waved again. David crept closer. He peered through the binoculars. Two startled eyes peered back at him. Two long brown ears stood straight up.

A rabbit. David's heart thumped. He'd seen

lots of pet rabbits but never a wild one. A wild rabbit was much better.

David tried to breathe quietly. The rabbit was watching him, but it didn't seem too afraid. He wished he'd saved a piece of hot dog bun. Then he remembered he'd stuck a chocolate chip cookie in his pocket. Slowly, he reached for it and broke off a piece. He held out his hand.

"Hey, little guy," he said. "Want some cookie?"

The rabbit twitched its nose.

"Come on," said David. "Nice cookie. Yum, yum."

He stretched his hand forward.

*Thump!* The rabbit stamped its feet and darted sideways. A quick flash of brown and it was gone.

"Rats!" said David. He stood up.

The clearing beside the creek was empty. Bradley's cap and bright red pack were disappearing around a bend in the trail. The other kids' voices sounded far away. David felt his heart jump. He stuffed his binoculars back in their case. He fumbled for his pack.

"Wait up, Bradley!" he hollered.

David raced down the trail.

Then he couldn't even see Bradley. And he couldn't hear anything, except the whistling of the wind in the tops of the pine trees.

# Chapter 8

# What If Bradley Tells?

David kept running.

His heart pounded. It hurt to breathe. He stopped beside a tall fir tree and hugged his chest with his arms.

Where was everyone?

David's eyes swam with tears. He swiped his hand across his face. He hunted wildly for landmarks. That dead tree with the branch sticking out — had he seen it before?

He couldn't remember. He hadn't been

paying that much attention. Not like Bradley, who had studied every tree and bush along the way.

David shivered. Bradley had been looking for bear tracks. That bear was probably wandering around right now, hunting for more stuff to eat.

A branch cracked in the bushes beside the trail. With a frightened yelp, David sped off again. His runners pounded on the hard ground.

The forest was a dark blur. A branch slapped across David's face and stung his cheek. His toe caught on something with a jerk. *Oooof!* He sprawled forward and hit the dirt with his hands and knees.

David lay on the ground for a minute, sucking in big gulps of air. Then he sat up with a moan and looked around. He had tripped on — a root! A dumb root. He hadn't even seen it. A slow, sickening feeling filled him. It was getting dark. Soon he wouldn't be able to see at all.

David stood up and brushed dirt and leaves off his knees.

*Chee, chee, chee.*

He spun around. A chipmunk.

He took a big breath. In class, when they'd talked about getting lost, Mr. Foster had said it was important not to panic. And, above all, to stay in one place.

The survival kit!

David opened his pack. He set his flashlight on the end of a log. He took out his survival kit and opened it with shaking fingers.

Band-Aids. David prodded his knees through his blue jeans. They stung but there was no blood coming through.

Granola bar. He was still stuffed from the cookout. Besides, he should save his food. What if he had to stay out all night?

David shuddered. He unfolded the orange garbage bag. Mr. Foster had said it would help people see you better. He tugged it over his head. The hole caught on his chin and tore. The plastic flapped against his knees.

David picked up his whistle. He blew it as hard as he could.

The chipmunk scrambled up a tree trunk. From the safety of a high branch, it chattered angrily. *Chee, chee, chee.*

It wasn't working. No one was coming. David took a big breath. He blew his whistle again.

Behind him, a branch cracked. He closed his eyes.

"Hi, Davey," said Bradley's voice.

David opened his eyes. He turned around. Bradley was standing in the middle of the trail. His face was red and his cap had tipped to one side.

"I had to go back to get my canteen," said Bradley. "I heard your whistle. You took a wrong turn in the trail."

"Oh," said David. His legs shook like jelly. He hoped Bradley wouldn't notice.

Bradley definitely noticed the orange garbage bag. He was staring right at it. David pulled the bag over his head and stuffed it in his pack. His cheeks burned. What if Bradley told the other kids? The story would spread around the whole school. Bradley didn't mind when kids laughed at him, but David did.

David followed Bradley silently along the trail. Bradley stopped beside the dead tree. "This is where you went wrong," he said.

He pointed one way. "That's the way back to where we had the cookout."

He pointed the other direction. "That goes back to the ranch."

"I get it," snapped David. Why did Bradley have to be the one to find him? It was just his rotten luck.

"I took an orienteering course in Cubs," said Bradley. "It helps you learn how to find your way around. I like the forest."

"I bet you don't like the forest at night," blurted David. He turned on his flashlight and flicked it in Bradley's face. "When it's *really* dark."

Bradley looked at the ground. David bit his lip. He wished he could take it back, but it was too late.

"Let's go," said Bradley in a stiff voice.

Bradley walked quickly. Sometimes he took a

few running steps. David hurried to keep up. He tried not to look at the dark shadows in the trees beside the trail.

In a few minutes, David saw the other kids' flashlights bobbing in a long wavy line. Thankfully, he slipped in behind Jason. His shoulders sagged with relief.

Jason turned around. "Where were you?" he demanded.

Some of the other kids turned around, too. David fiddled with the switch on his flashlight. His heart thumped. He'd look like such a dope. Would Bradley keep his mouth shut?

Bradley said, "We stopped to look at some bear tracks."

"What?" said Lesley and Sarah. Their eyes widened.

Everyone stared at David and Bradley. David's legs felt wobbly with relief. He tried not to look surprised. Inside, he felt like laughing.

For a second, Jason's eyes flickered with envy. Then he scowled and muttered, "I bet."

\* \* \*

When they got back to the ranch, Mrs. Foster was waiting with mugs of hot chocolate. Jason and David and some of the other kids carried their mugs down to the river and sat on rocks.

David listened while the kids talked in low voices about the midnight feast. He poked at the marshmallow floating in his mug. He fished it out and gave it to Jason. He didn't think he'd ever be able to eat another marshmallow in his life.

Jason licked the goo off his fingers. He said, "What was that weird thing you were going to tell us about Bradley?"

Matt and Jonathan stopped licking their marshmallows and listened. David looked back at the house. Bradley was standing in the light by the porch, waiting for seconds of hot chocolate.

David bit his lip. How could he tell on Bradley now? He'd feel like a jerk. He was positive everyone could hear his heart hammering inside his jacket. "There isn't anything. I just made it up."

"Hey, come on," said Jason.

"I did," said David. He looked Jason right in the eye. "Honest."

Jason slurped the last of his hot chocolate. "You're the one who's weird," he muttered in disgust.

David picked up a rock and threw it into the water. He was glad he hadn't told Bradley's secret. But he hoped Jason wouldn't ask again.

# Chapter 9

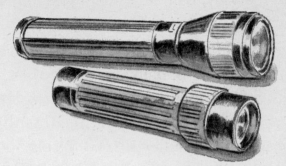

# A Noise in the Night

Mr. Foster went over the nighttime rules. "No loud voices, no horseplay and absolutely NO leaving the tents after lights-out."

Some of the kids looked sideways at each other and giggled. David pretended not to notice. He wished they hadn't picked Bradley's tent for the midnight feast.

A few minutes later, David and Bradley crawled into their tent. David decided to sleep in his T-shirt and jeans. He slid into his sleeping bag. It felt cool and slippery.

Bradley thrashed around noisily. He changed into his pajamas. He dug into his backpack and took out a package of cookies. He slid the cookies inside his sleeping bag and crawled in.

David turned off his flashlight. After a minute, Bradley turned his off, too. David tried to look at his hand in the dark. Through the thin tent walls, he could see Mr. Foster's flashlight bobbing through the trees.

Mr. Foster's flashlight faded away. David heard muffled giggles from another tent. Bradley crunched loudly on a cookie.

It was darker than the bear den. Much darker. Bradley stopped crunching cookies. He lay very still. David propped himself up on his elbow and stared into the darkness beside him. All he could see of Bradley was a darker shape.

Bradley gave a big sigh. After a minute, he made little nibbling sounds, like a mouse eating bits of cracker. David lay back and closed his eyes. Maybe no one was coming for the midnight feast, after all. Maybe Bradley was the only one who was going to eat. David rolled over on his other side.

Someone giggled outside the tent door. A light flashed in David's eyes.

Bradley sat up and blinked like an owl. A piece of cookie stuck to his chin. "What's going on?"

"We're coming in," hissed Jason.

The boys and girls crowded into the tent. David pulled up the bottom of his sleeping bag to make room for everyone. He could smell Cheesies and pretzels. Yuck.

Everyone looked at each other and giggled. Lesley opened a can of pop. It made a hissing sound. Fizzy cola splattered on David's sleeping bag.

"Hey!" said David.

"Shhh!" said Lesley and Sarah. They giggled.

David chose half an oatmeal cookie. He tried to chew quietly. He hoped Mr. Foster couldn't hear them.

Jason stuck the end of his flashlight in his mouth. His cheeks glowed like a jack-o'-

lantern. He took the flashlight out and said, "Want to hear a ghost story?"

David shivered. He wriggled deeper into his sleeping bag.

"Once there was this guy called . . . called . . . Bradley."

"This is going to be boring," said Lesley.

"Let me finish," said Jason. "Well, Bradley was in this big old mansion one night. He was just sitting there . . . eating . . . um . . . doughnuts. And then he heard footsteps outside the door. They were coming closer and closer."

Jason leaned forward.

"Cloooooser and clooooser. And then the doorknob turned. And a voice said, 'Bradley, oh, Braaad-ley, I'm coming to get you.' "

David looked at Bradley. He was eating a Cheesie and grinning.

"This is dumb," said Matt. "And it's not scary."

"I have a story," said Bradley. "This is true. It happened when I was camping with the Cubs."

Jason groaned loudly.

"I saw a grizzly bear."

Everyone stared at Bradley.

Jason said, "That's not a ghost story."

Bradley ignored him. "The grizzly was just disappearing into the bushes. It had a silvery hump on its back."

"Yeah, and you followed its tracks, right?" said Jason in disgust.

"No," said Bradley. "But I saw it."

"Were you scared?" said Sarah.

"No," said Bradley.

David lay back and wrote his name on the roof of the tent with his flashlight. He wished Bradley would stop talking about grizzly bears. He wished the midnight feast would end and everyone would leave.

*Crack!*

*Thump!*

David sat up with a jerk. Cold prickles crawled up his back. He stared at the door of the tent.

"Did you hear that?" squeaked Sarah.

David swallowed. "What was it?" he whispered.

*Thump!*

*Thud!*

"There's something out there," said Jason. His face was white.

Jonathan closed his eyes. "We're dead," he whispered.

*Crack!*

Everyone jumped. Matt dropped the bag of Cheesies. Lesley spilled her can of cola. David felt the pop seep through his sleeping bag onto his leg.

"Uh-oh," moaned Matt. "What are we going to do?"

A funny look spread across Jason's face. He said in a shaky voice, "Bradley is the animal expert here. Right? So why doesn't he go and find out what it is?"

David gasped. Go outside in the middle of the night? In the dark?

"Forget it," said Bradley.

*Thump!*

*Crack!*

The kids stared at each other. David gripped

the top of his sleeping bag. He wanted to crawl right to the bottom.

"It's okay," said Bradley. "There's nothing out there that can hurt you. I know that."

"So prove it," said Jason.

Bradley stared at Jason for a long time.

Jason's eyes glinted. "I dare you."

Bradley sucked in his breath. He leaned forward and unzipped the tent door.

David wanted to shout, "You don't have to go!"

The words stuck in his throat. He poked at the wet circle on his sleeping bag. He didn't look at Bradley.

Bradley slipped through the tent door. He held his flashlight like a sword. He disappeared into the darkness. David hugged his arms to his chest. He felt cold and shivery. And he couldn't hear anything now.

"He'll come back in a minute," said Jason. "You'll see."

No one felt like eating. Sarah crumpled up her pretzel bag. The crackling sound in the quiet tent made David jump.

After a long time, Lesley whispered, "I don't think Bradley's coming back."

"He didn't *have* to go," said Jason. His cheeks were red. His voice shook.

David realized that everyone was looking at him. He spoke slowly. "He'll be okay. Bradley can do a lot of stuff. He knows about animals. And he can find his way around."

"He's pretty brave," said Matt. "He's not scared of bears."

But he *is* scared of the dark, thought David.

David made up his mind. He slipped his jacket over his T-shirt.

Jason's mouth fell open. "Where are you going?"

David took a big breath. "To find Bradley."

Jason stared at him. His eyes looked like black marbles in his white face. He said in a trembling voice, "It's my fault he's out there. I'm coming, too."

# Chapter 10

# Way to Go, Bradley

David and Jason huddled outside the tent. David waved his flashlight in a big circle. The trees looked like tall black shadows. Something fluttered past their faces.

"A bat!" squeaked Jason.

David shuddered. "Come on," he said. "This way."

The boys stumbled along the path to the house.

"Ow!" said Jason. "I stubbed my toe."

"Shhh," hissed David.

He stepped on a branch and jumped at the sharp crack. His hands felt clammy. He peered around nervously. Where was Bradley?

"Hey," said Jason. "What was that?"

David stopped walking. Jason bumped into his back. "What was *what?*" whispered David.

"I heard something," said Jason.

David stared into the darkness. There *was* something out there. They'd all heard it. A stick snapped and a rock clattered over the ground. David pointed his flashlight along the path. Something white flapped toward the boys. A light floated beside it. The back of David's neck prickled. A ghost!

David heard Jason suck in his breath. David picked up a stick. He pointed one end at the ghost.

"Don't shoot!" said Bradley's voice. "It's me."

David looked at Bradley's baggy white pajamas. They flapped like wings around his legs.

"Whew," said Bradley. He squinted in the bright light from David's flashlight. "Would you mind shining that somewhere else?"

"Sorry," said David. He pointed the light at the ground. He could hear Bradley's teeth chattering.

"I found out what was making the noise," said Bradley. "It was that deer. I chased it out of Mrs. Foster's rose garden!"

David's legs felt like porridge. But he couldn't help grinning. If Bradley said he chased a deer, he probably did.

Jason didn't say, "I bet." He didn't say, "Yeah, right." He said, "Way to go, Bradley!"

"I was really scared at first," admitted Bradley. "But it's okay out here now."

David knew what Bradley meant. Camping didn't seem scary anymore, not with Bradley and Jason along. The boys were still for a minute. An owl hooted and dark wings flapped silently over their heads.

David swept his flashlight along the river. It looked like a black snake. Then he pointed the flashlight to the opposite shore. He stiffened. "Look!" he gasped.

Jason and Bradley shone their flashlights on the river, too.

A huge black animal stood at the edge of the water. It waded on its long legs for a few steps and then bent over to drink.

"It's a bull moose," whispered Bradley.

The boys watched in silence. The moose lifted its head. Water streamed from its muzzle. Its great antlers gleamed in the light.

"Moose are the biggest land animals in North America, next to bison," Bradley whispered. "They can weigh nearly three times as much as a black bear."

David sucked in his breath. He could feel his heart hammering inside his chest.

"Can moose swim?" whispered Jason.

Bradley cleared his throat. "Moose are very good swimmers. They can swim up to sixteen kilometres at a time. And they can run fifty-five kilometres an hour," he said.

Bradley would know. David licked his lips.

The river wasn't very wide. And with those long legs, the moose could probably wade right across. A little bit of David wanted to run. He kept his eyes glued on the moose.

The moose walked back onto the shore. It nibbled the tips of a low bush. It chewed slowly and watched the boys. David felt a wobbly grin spread across his face. He couldn't wait to tell his mom and dad.

Branches cracked and voices giggled behind the boys. A light bobbed in the trees. The moose raised its head. It made a grunting sound that made goose bumps prickle the back of David's neck. Then it turned and loped into the forest.

"Here come the others," said Jason. He sounded disappointed. "That was the best thing I ever saw," he added softly.

David let his breath out slowly. He knew what Jason meant. He closed his eyes tightly. He wanted to save the picture of the moose.

A gust of wind rustled the leaves. David opened his eyes and took a deep breath of the cool night air. It smelled like pine needles and grass and river. He reached into his jacket pocket and pulled out his jumbo fruit and nut chocolate bar.

"Yes!" said Jason.

"Yum!" cried Bradley. "Hurray for Davey!"

David looked Bradley straight in the eyes. "My friends call me David," he said firmly.

He waited until the others joined them. Then he broke his chocolate bar into pieces and gave everyone a chunk. But the piece with the most nuts and raisins — he gave to Bradley!

## Becky Citra

Becky Citra lives in Bridge Lake, British Columbia, with her husband and daughter. Their ranch is often visited by moose, bears and coyotes!

Becky is also the author of *My Homework Is in the Mail!* When she's not writing, she likes to spend time outdoors — camping, hiking, riding or cross-country skiing.